THE PUNCH CLOCK DRAGON

Poetic Ru
Thinker, T

"Nouveau Louvre (Escalier du Pavillon Mollien)" Édouard Baldus Digital image courtesy of Getty's Open Content Program.

Explanations:

Back in my teenage years, I became the forever GM for an ongoing D&D game amongst my friends. We started while we were in 9th Grade, playing in my friend's parents' basement. I had some strange ability to make little dramas with dice and mutual imagining people very much enjoyed participating in. I was always walking backwards laying down tracks of stories for people to follow. It was this experience that feeds my novel writing (such as it is) and helped me create the world of Trithofar, in which most of my novels are or will be set. And due to my supposed talent in making up stories as we went along, one of the Thomases in our gaming group called me 'Plotspider.' This has since become my moniker and a permanent part, I think, of my brand. This picture you see below was found on FLICKR.com, and is covered by Creative Commons License; however, I will do the right thing and attribute it to Patrick Kavanagh. I love jumping spiders the most, and I am grateful to find this picture.

This book is the result of years of thinking on paper my thoughts, forming them up into poetry or ramblings like a lackadaisical drill sergeant never anticipating a war, but sometimes waking up his wordish beings to drill and ready to be sent out into the world to make of it what they will, only to tell them again 'as you were.' Having arrived at the first writer's conference I've ever attended at the local library encouraged me to actually publish this collection of my works. Let's see if my poems go anywhere or do anything.

My poems are somewhat like me: random, rambling, semi-profound. They are reflections of the odd angle through which I look at the world, and they bespeak my strange, possibly autistic, mind, my faith, and quite often, my dreams and memories. As for the title of this book? I'll let the poem I'm referencing speak to that. Suffice it to say, I love fantasy quite a bit, and fancy myself to become a novelist in that genre, but find myself forced to acknowledge reality, despite my better judgment.

These poems have not been curated in any particular order, except the order they were recorded in Google Docs, recovered like ancient ships from old notebooks full of stains and crinkles and pen scratches.

DEDICATION:

To properly dedicate this book would require another poem. However, this book is dedicated to all the people in my life. Full stop. So many of my family and so many friends have inspired and encouraged poetry from me. I'll specifically mention my friends like Dave (Benedict), Will, both the Thomases, Patrick, Mark (all of them), Mike, Lily, and all the teachers crazy enough to work with me. To the teachers who inspired me, such as Mrs. Buckhalt, Mrs. Roach, Mr. Spain, Dr. Bertolet, Dr. Carroll, Dr. Gresham, and of course, Dr. Hannah, I thank you for making teaching look so easy, and poetry so interesting, and for not letting me know the truth until it was too late. I will further dedicate this book to my parents, Jim and Judy. And finally, to my lovely Lacy, and my wondrous daughters, Lily, Naomi, and Julianna. All of you have inspired poetry, and I hope you enjoy what you have started bubbling up inside my head.

Table of Contents

Explanations: 2
DEDICATION: 4
"Is Poetry Here Today?" 8
"Anointing" 9
"Cellular Springtime" 10
"Returning to the Sea" 11
"Song of Sancho" 13
"Howling at the Moon" 14
"Clorvitis" 15
"Outside" 16
"Little Curses" 17
"The Library After Dark" 18
"The Frog of Time" 19
"Echo" 20
"IPhone Emperors" 21
"Yard Work" 23
"The Lonely" 25
"Voice Crime" 26
"Ant Lies" 27
"Passion Is the Wild Inside" 28
"The Demon's Game" 30
"I Live Between" 31
"Nightfall" 32
"The Stars Upon the Hill" 33
"Haiku Around The Lake" 34
"A Brief Comparison of Trees" 35
"Invisible Squirrel" 36
"Dying Tree Struck By Lightning" 37
"Spider" 38

"My Brother is in Heaven Now" 39
"The Fourth of July" 40
"Prayer Upon Hearing an Ambulance" 41
"Filibustering" 42
"When Comes the Hand of God" 44
"Sing a Song of Rain" 45
"Don't Fear the Wounding" 46
"The House" 47
"Blazé" 50
"The City" 51
"Gun In The Night" 53
"His Last Blink" 55
"I Saw a Cloud Like an Angel" 60
"Apologia" 61
"My Peculiar Curse" 63
"Frustrated Teacher Rant" 64
"Watching a Band At 8th And Rail Bar After 66
Chaperoning the Prom: 2014, I Think." 66
"A Ladybug Smell" 68
"In Search of Poetry" 69
"Who's Never Studied Star Wars" 71
"No Music is Playing." 73
"Ancestor Homosapien" 74
"Save Them" 76
"Love Among the Dead" 77
"True Story: Nightmare 5/12/15" 78
"If I Did, Would You?" 79
"Like Many Birds" 80
"Tea Party" 81
"God's Real Language Is Poetry" 82
"A Punch Clock Dragon" 83

"Why Teachers Hoard" 84

"Night Clock" 85

"The Game of Ku" 86

"I am Dead, but Lesson Plans are Due" 89

"Elegy for Lilly Marie Gullage" 90

"Another Dream Poem: Dad CSI" 91

"A Joke Poem?" 91

"Hope This Helps" 92

"Woven Universe" 93

"Random Tanka" 94

"Ivy is Convoluted" 95

"Upon Investigating A Sun-Shadow Mandala Project" 96

"Head over Heels" 97

"If You Fall Into A River" 97

"The Wasted Light" 98

"Let's Play" 99

"For Fields and Flowers" 99

"A Window Casement" 100

"But, I love…" 101

"Artists Unlike Me" 103

"Is Poetry Here Today?"

Is poetry here today?
Does it hide inside my pen?
Or wait upon the page?
Michelangelo thought
His marble already hid a statue,
Awaiting revelation within.
Is poetry like that?
Is it already on my paper now,
Or buried behind my laptop screen?
Or maybe I'm the marble,
Hard, unshaped, waiting.
If so,
What must be carved away to get it out?
What must be cut to make art of me?

"Anointing"

My infant daughter shoves her fingers
Into her mouth until they are covered
With her shining spit.
She smiles and wipes her hand,
Not gently, down my cheek,
And across my nose,
Into my beard.
She leaves trails
And
I am anointed.
She wipes approval
Across my face.
She dries it with the bright beams
From bright blue eyes
And her pink, gummy grin.
She is putting warpaint on me.
The fluttering hand
And the smile behind it
Seal my heart.
"You are my champion,"
They tell me.
"You go before me.
You go with me.
You will fight for me.
It will not be easy.
I will not make it easy."
She tangles her fingers
Into my beard and pulls.
I smile when it stings my cheek.
I never had a choice, Princess.
I never wanted one.

"Cellular Springtime"

In a tan, drab classroom,
A gray, lonely winter, cold,
Peeked inside a smudgy window,
To watch us all wrapped in coats.
A strange Springtime awoke.
The professor's call for break
Sent apparently a warm zeitgeber,
To shifting chrysa-like bodies.
And all at once
Electric equinox.
Flowers with petals like moonlight
Grew on stalks of flesh,
They bloomed warm and bright.
They sent invisible, infectious pollen spores,
Seeds of thought
Into allergic, itching ears.
All around me in the room,
Cups of coffee steamed like melting ice,
Baby bird beeps and bee buzzes
Were alive in the air.
Fifteen minutes.
The season died sharply,
Skipped over summertime and fall,
Retired, and winter was back.
The butterflies wrapped back in their cocoons.
The flowers back in their earthlike pockets.
Pages lay open like snowy fields again.
The wind of the professor back again,
Blowing dancing snow crystals
Into our thoughts again:
Cold, sometimes bitter,
But biting and stinging
The living flesh.

"Returning to the Sea"

We return ever softer to the sea.
When we are young
Our parents must call and pull us back
From the hungry riptide waiting
To devour the foolish hearts
Of childhood.
The salt water burns our eyes
And the jelly tentacles
Sting our ankles like fire.
The sand finds its way
Into crevices and secret places
And it sprinkles our toes
Like the sugar on donuts.
Every white gull born aloft
On the breaths of sunrise
Has a call for us
Little wisdoms only children know.

> A little time, a little wear
> And we return slower now.
> As teens, we ponder the number of times
> God really counted the grains of powder
> *Phlimphing* underfoot.
> We trace the hems of bathing suits
> With our eyes, calculating the difference
> Between the fiery cloth and the flesh like fire.
> Our feet tolerate as best they may
> The ocean lapping, licking them.
> No more sand castles built between us
> But we admire their ruin in the evening
> Where the savage crabs fight over flotsam
> In the pink last minutes of daylight.
> We hold hands together, strolling the strand
> Thinking we've conquered life,
> Not ready yet to challenge beer and lobster.

> And then we return again to the sea,

Sometimes without bathing suits at all,
T-shirts and shorts instead,
Dripping with tedious applications
Of sunscreen we had to help each other smear.

If the sea is lucky it gets us to our hips.
And that's cold enough, far enough.
We don't get stung anymore,
Because we don't immerse our heads,
And we stand high enough to see the jelly ungulate.
We tell our children to build sand castles
"Because it's fun," we say to them
When what we mean is "safe."
Such dreams don't take us to the water.
We've abdicated thrones of imagined kingdoms.
We nod at the sea now, wanting only to visit.
We eat shrimp and call it good,
Like God must have done
When he first pinched one gray bug to life.
We scorn the teenage screaming.
We came here to teach ourselves
To long for getting back to work
So when we go, we want to be.

We return ever, ever softer to the sea,
Like children moved out of state.
Now upon returning, we don't really return.
Our feet never touch the water,
And the wind calls to those gone deaf.
"The sea hasn't changed" we say
And the sea says the same of us.
We laugh at the grandchildren
Building their castles
Because they thought it fun.
We call to the children to be careful
To stay out of the water:
"You might drown."

The Punch Clock Dragon Sighs by Jared Gullage

"Song of Sancho"

Behold my Master Don Quixote
And how he sits upon his steed.
He rides and fights across the plains
And performs his noble deeds.
How strange, how odd, how frightful 'tis
A man of noble birth and age,
With love for mad chivalric code,
Seek havoc with sudden rage.
His foes be mills or giants vicious,
Or wizard curse mysterious,
Fight on, fight on, my master, great
Quixote, fierce and serious.

So ride on Rocinante's back
Dulcinea's champion choice.
By God may we be richly blessed
May vict'ry's cry be in your voice.
The knightly tasks are ne'er complete
And onwards we will ever ride
Our lives with troubles are replete,
And duty brings a pained backside.
I hope I prove myself to you,
I hope you find me worthy, Lord.
And when your sword you lay aside,
I'll get my island as a reward.

The Punch Clock Dragon Sighs by Jared Gullage

"Howling at the Moon"

A cowboy camping by a river stayed up and observed the night.
As he sipped some coffee, he listened to a wolf howling in moonlight.
Soon the man drank up his coffee, and he listened to the cry.
The wolf continued yelping, and the cowboy wondered why.
So he left the campfire's comforts and went searching through the night.
His only guides were the lonesome cries and the heavenly bodies' light.
He found the wolf on a mountainside, and he interrupted his mournful song
To inquire of him the answers to the questions he'd had for so long.
"The moon and stars are shining high, and the wind whispers 'cross the plains.
On such a lovely evening as this, what reason have you to complain?"
The wolf stopped howling then, and to face the man, turned 'round.
Before he decided to answer him, he decided to sit himself down.
The wolf looked sleepily at the cowboy, but heard his question clearly,
And not long past before he responded to his query.
With one of his large and hairy paws he pointed to the clear night sky.
"You see that cursed moon up there? That's the reason for our cry."
The cowboy was confused, but let the wolf continue the speech,
And he explained to the curious man a fact both strange and unique.
"Every time that moon is full, you see, it shines up there so big and bright,
And since out here there are no trees it keeps us awake all night.
If the choice was ever ours to make, we'd rather be asleep right now,
But since that infernal moon stays up, our frustration makes us howl.
So we stay awake the entire night long, singing to that rude satellite,
Hoping and praying the entire time that it just might go to sleep tonight.
The cowboy laughed and said, "I sleep in a tent and never realized
How big a problem the moon can be, but now I do and truly sympathize.
I feel sorry for you, but I'm getting tired, so I guess our talk must end.
I hope you find your peace and quiet, and get the rest you need, my friend."
The wolf grew angry and attacked and pinned the cowboy to the dirt.
He bit, clawed, growled and snarled and left the cowboy badly hurt.
He then loped down the mountainside, and he found the campsite.
After going in the cowboy's tent, the wolf never howled again that night.

The Punch Clock Dragon Sighs by Jared Gullage

"Clorvitis"

If I went down the street one day
And said "I have Clorvitis."
I wonder how many women would shrink
As though what followed was: "It's contagious?"
How many times would people hasten away
Or raise hands to lips as though to hide
Their delicate lives from my infection?
How many children would giggle and point?
How long would it take kids today
To find a wicked rhyme to mock my shame?
How many men would simply walk away
Hands deep in pockets to be washed?
Quite a few, I'd bet, would self-righteously say:
"It's your own fault for living like you do."

If I asked them all: "Do you have a clorvitis?"
Then, what now might they all say to me?
The women might be quite shocked at this
As though I requested their belt and slacks.
The elders would perhaps raise hands against me
As though I had become a public danger.
The children would hide behind their parents,
Point at me, and maybe shriek: "He's a stranger!"
Some men, I suppose, must glare anger at me,
And some would pretend they understood.
And what disgusted looks others would give.
There would be some to gasp and turn away,
Using their hands to cover their minds.
If I told them: "Clorvitis is not even a word."
I dare say that only one or two would hear.
How many would understand the test?

"Outside"

Round and round we run
Out in the grasses and beneath the stars,
Not going anywhere further than thirty yards
From home but actually seeing everything.
Round and round we run
Never leaving the backyard
But putting on armor sweatshirts,
Screaming at the top of our lungs,
Fighting dragons and monsters
Whose bones are made of branches
With swords forged of hickory steel.
Round and round we run
Never leaving the hawk eyed watching
Of a mother always silently checking, but
Still we leave this planet for a distant world,
Turning rocks and trees into spaceships,
Seeing aliens made of wind and we make
Lasers out of water pistols always assuming
That all the monsters want to kill us,
And destroy the castle or home planet
That we would die to protect
By laying down on the grass
And laughing.

"Little Curses"

Bitter curses bite my heel
Just enough to sting me;
Not enough to make me fall,
Only enough to bring me
To a stumbling pace when
I'm running quickest forth,
Just enough to stump my toe
When I open up the door.
Opportunities come my way
But all of them with cost.
The sweetness of every gain
Always salted with a loss.

"The Library After Dark"

An ancient tome closes somewhere,
A cough, maybe years old, reaches my ears
Laughter at the door and hands on glass,
As the door opens and they step out.
A hammering of stamping upon the pulp
A creak of spines and crack of knuckles
Scratching pencil lead shrinks upon a page
While somewhere a mind screams in sighs
And fingers knot up in slightly grayer hair,
And a hiss comes from the sliding glasses.
Cars are whispering in the wind outside.
One light above me is forgetting lines
And stammering out the hummed lullaby
That the others already know by heart.
In the distance, someone uses precious air
Does not speak it, but lets it fly through teeth
As someone picks up the wind and carries it
Silently through his thoughts and out again.

Inspired by visiting the Auburn University Library, one cold evening.

"The Frog of Time"

My time on Earth is like a frog
Who jumps occasionally heavenward
And splats down again upon its belly,
And croaks with laughter and pain.
Up and down, legs awkwardly *splaggling*.
I'm heading for the edge of murky waters.
Somehow, when I'm there,
And under those pollen-covered depths,
I'll speed into clouds of forgotten.
Deeper, dimmer, darker, vanished.
Out again, out again when it's time for song,
Out again, out again the birds and snakes are gone.

"Echo"

"Ha!" I laughed a laugh
That echoed far away.
Into the woods around me
A warning broke the day.
A man had wandered out.
Birds flew, squirrels hid,
In branches of their trees.
A man was laughing.
With my single outburst
I marked the breeze
I stood my ground
I laughed at the world
Made it kowtow around.
But, you see,
It was, to me,
Hypocrisy.

I was never really laughing.

"IPhone Emperors"

Are we not little emperors
Who summon onto the stage
With disinterested mouths
And spoiled fingers -
With the least movement of which
We expect absolute obedience -
Songs and film
To come dancing?

We expect our entertainers waiting in the wings,
Harps in hand, tongues scratching out rehearsals.
"Come when called or anger me!"
"Dance, Movie, dance!"
"Sing, captured lyrics, sing to me!"
"Make me happy!"
We are little princelings,
Each with a pocket kingdom
Filled with dancing puppets.

We claim to own Music,
To keep Her in our pocket's cage,
Like beanstalk giants with enchanted harps,
To become incensed if She won't play.
We pay for Her company cheaply,
Take her down from the block,
Naked and branded for Her work
To dance in our audacious ears.

When Her prison be swept clear,
And the evidence of her bower gone,
We rave at those slave masters
Who first caged Her and let her go.
We demand recompense for Her escape.

This pervades us.
At least, it has lurked in me.
When I think this way,
I like better the thought of radios,
Meeting Music in a chance encounter,
While I happen to be along my way,
As a pleasant and occasional stranger,
She sings her secrets to my sleeping heart,
And walks freely away again with my thanks.
I hope to follow Her, and now to simply listen
When She sings again,
And in grace, She can turn and smile
And freely make me happy.

"Yard Work"

My Dad and I found a driveway today.
We carved it out of some leaves in the yard.
With the leaf blower, I discovered it,
And Dad did the detail work with a rake,
Trimming the outer edges neatly.
Then, afterwards, Dad and I got axes,
And together turned tree trunks
Into slivers,
And later, of those, we made fire.

That evening, we shackled ourselves
To the necks of Rottweilers
Who dragged us, our arms stretched,
From streetlight to streetlight,
Sniffing and huffing.

We sat down in the cool of evening
And together ignited the television,
Watching its blaze, but not really.
We both held as much interest for it,
As someone might a campfire,
Watching, but not really watching,
Basking in its inconsequential glow,
But never questioning the flickers,

Together, my father and I sat at the table,
Eating my mother's country fried steak,
Lamenting our battle wounds from the day,
Reminding ourselves of how
The leaves will bury the driveway again,
And the dogs will need walking again,
And more trees will fall and need chopping.

We think about Saturdays.
Saturday will come again and again.
We say we will be there to greet them
That every weekend will wake us.
We deny secretly they won't.

"The Lonely"

Loneliness is when small talk
Becomes so desperate
A man drills himself
In his heaviest coat
To remember the name
Of a total stranger at a bus stop merely because
He is tired of staring
At mud puddles
And hearing bus brakes
Hissing as he gets in.

Loneliness is when a man can stand completely isolated
Among five thousand,
Crowded are his fears
In his mind
At midnight,
Clinging to the faces who smiled
As their owners melt
Into slicks of memory.

It is a depth,
A dark,
A cold,
So enclosing
Every single word spoken through it
Echoes like
Cave-born droplets,
And sounds like love.

The unkind words people speak upon turning
Away and forgetting,
Fall like axes,
Amputating
The lonely shadow
From the heel.

Every time the lonely stops in front of his door again,
The question
Opens to him.
He asks himself:
Will I get up
Tomorrow?
Will any care
If I don't?

The Punch Clock Dragon Sighs by Jared Gullage

"Voice Crime"

A man standing before me
Shot words out his mouth
And filled his loved ones
Full of bloody holes.
He watched them wriggle
Falling back against the wall
Like victims in a mob movie.
He stood over the corpses
Watched them bleed
Sometimes double-tapping,
Two in the heart, one in the head,
Before leaving my bathroom,
And my bathroom's mirror.
This man clicked the safety,
Put his mouth in its holster,
Concealed it under his coat.

I walked out into daylight,
And convinced everyone
I was good enough.

"Ant Lies"

If humans were like ants
We'd talk with our smells.
Honesty might smell like sweat

Or maybe like farts?
Perfumes and musks,
Colognes and mouthwashes
Would be more attractive words,
But they'd be lies.

So, when we were telling the truth,
We'd stink and run people away.
When we told honey-covered lies,
Everyone would want to hear them.
Could people really live like this?

"Passion Is the Wild Inside"

Passion is the little strong man
Inside each one of us who
When the heart tries to collapse
Stretches and pushes it back out.
Passion is a hand left open,
Waiting to close again,
To take hold of a yet unknown,
Captivated quarry.
Passion is a living seed planted
In fertile ground anxious
To grow through cement and stone
And lap up rivers of rain.
Passion is an angry hornet seeing
The larger enemy throwing rocks
Stinging the unguarded side of hope
With a tiny drop of venom.
Passion is a hurricane,
A storm barely kept from shore,
Whose winds just touch a sail
Too terrified to fully grasp it.
Passion is a place untamed,
Ground trampled by wild horses,
A grass valley accustomed to quaking
Below mountains clothed in cloud.
Passion is an arrow drawn back
Held by quivering, aching fingers,
The archer tense and ready
To take his venison or die.
Passion is the wild mustang,
Flaunting his painted sides,
Across an open, Indian prairie,
Not caring if there is wolf or man,
Letting his hooves speak for it.
Passion is the sight of beauty,
A hand waiting above another hand

A smile waiting above another smile
That place where sparks are made
Between two so close
An infinity slips through,
That desperate land between
One choice and another,
A dwindling distance between
Hand and hand.

"The Demon's Game"

The demon's game is not to forge a deal then break it,
But to snicker in the dark at the foolish hearts who make it.
He knows his terms, these darkest dealers, it is no gamble.
It is the unlocking of a gate to start the wisher's ramble.
The Hell-spawn minion given power to command
Has no worry what's written with his contracting hand.
He knows full well the wandering hearts of every man
Will bring him back for better and more grand.
He'll exhaust his dreams and run ragged his desires,
And voluntarily double down to risk all Hell's fires.

"I Live Between"

I live between many things
Between the cold winds
And the fires
Between the lost
And things yet desired
Between things not ripe
And things not rotten
Things not yet found
And things yet forgotten
I live between many things
Between grace and sin
Between without and within
I live between many things
Between love and hate
Birth of life, choice of fate
Not quite fully covered
Not really all that nude
Almost sick and half cured
Cultivated and left crude.
I live the life between
Walking on top of fences
Or hopping on the green
Between a day remembered
And one lived in dreams.
Between thirst and a cup
Seconds had, seconds offered,
Down and up.
My life resides there
In between.

"Nightfall"

Marching against the winds,
The trees put on their funeral robes,
And carry the casket onwards.
The horizon is set ablaze now,
By the mighty torch of heaven.
An appropriate funeral pyre flames
On the top of distant wood waiting.
The reeds whisper secrets to each other,
Like the children who don't know
That it's a sober and quiet moment.
Timid stars now turn on their lanterns,
The pale moon raises his face,
Opens the scripture, preparing to read.
A strange choir has assembled,
Singing a peculiar and solemn melody
"The time has come at last," they sing,
"We can only now remember Today."
For such a death all have come to mourn.
Time is gone, and it shall never be reborn.

"The Stars Upon the Hill"

How bright the stars shine upon this hill.
They are flaming spirits none can kill,
And bright orbs, which the heavens, do fill.
How bright the stars shine upon this hill.

How wide the moon's grin, looking down.
Behold, it smiles upon all the ground.
And bright, silver light shines all around.
How wide the moon's grin, looking down.

How quiet and still the forests do seem,
Dark and deep as though from a dream.
On the dewy leaves, moonlight gleams.
How quiet and still the forests do seem.

How solemn the ancient mountains stand
As the midnight guardians of the land.
Somber, sober, shadowy yet grand,
How solemn the ancient mountains stand.

How radiant your lovely eyes before me are,
Capturing mountains, woods, moon, and stars.
They embrace and caress my love-filled heart.
How radiant your lovely eyes before me are.

How pleasant it is to love and hold you near
And to share a love that is lasting and dear.
How beautiful the night is because you're here.
How pleasant it is to love and hold you near.

"Haiku Around The Lake"

The water is still
Reflecting sunlight like glass
The movement of life.

The leaves are still green
As though they will never fall
Nor ever be gold

Spider hangs alone.
Spinning all his time away
Trying to survive.

The winds speak to trees
Gently caressing the limbs,
Imparting secrets.

The duck is paddling,
Swimming steadfast on the lake,
Cutting the surface.

Bats climbing under stars
Wings flailing haphazardly
Beautiful klutzes.

Lake surface swirling,
Fish snapping at drowning bugs.
They're gone forever.

Locusts are singing,
Their singing is an anthem
Hail coming darkness.

Walking leaves footprints
Standing leaves only one mark
Silent memory.

The Punch Clock Dragon Sighs by Jared Gullage

"A Brief Comparison of Trees"

Is a dead tree
Standing a hundred feet tall
Proud of its achievements?

                                                    Is a young sapling,
                                                    Barely there at all,
                                              Aware of its existence?

"Invisible Squirrel"

Invisible Squirrel, I believe you're there,
I hear you calling in the morning air.
I hear your claws tightly dug in a tree
I hear the acorns falling close to me.
I believe you exist; I know not where.
Invisible squirrel, I think you're there.
As of just now, you live in the lore
Of scratching sounds in sycamore.
Invisible squirrel, I know you're there,
I can hear you calling in the sunset air.

"Dying Tree Struck By Lightning"

A lightning bolt smashed that tree,
And the wind finished it off.
The bark is shredded.
The trunk broke in half.
Parts of its heart are now
Exposed, violated, burnt open
By an ancient, summer storm.

                             Still a branch emerges,
                              Trying to salvage it all.
                      A tiny, scraggly, childish reach,
                    Trying to save fifty feet of dying,
            And a hundred years of growth abandoned.

That is hope.

"Spider"

Cocoons, all wrapped tightly,
Filled with preservative poisons,
Waiting in line,
For the one who has trapped them
To rip through them
And devour their innards.

I remove one
From the cold waiting darkness,
But leave the rest for later,
And the refrigerator closes.

"My Brother is in Heaven Now"

I know my brother is in heaven now,
Because I'm sure he knew of God.
He rarely worshiped enclosed in walls,
But prayed in woods in which he trod.

The roof upon his sanctuary was
The limbs of trees and all their leaves.
The birds which flew around him then,
Were choirs with praise-filled melodies.

His church possessed no stained-glass,
Nor any windows, doors, no locks at all.
The sunset light across the sky,
Sufficed to form his temple's walls.

Where'er he sat to rest his mud-stained feet
Would serve as good as any pew.
He got a baptism within
The flowing streams or new-formed dew.

I picture him quiet now,
The breath of God upon the wind.
I think that while it thunders here
The Lord speaks peaceful words to him.

"The Fourth of July"

Sulfuric smoke rises now
From Black Cats and sparklers,
Instead of the dragon-maws
Of the roaring black cannons.
The charred flesh smell rising
Now prevalent among the neighbors,
Is a barbecue roasting ribs,
Instead of people who fall dead
Lying on broken bayonets
And forgotten dreams of home.
The cries of war come not now
From great generals and officers,
But from children in the yard
Pretending to be British or Yank,
Or another *glorious* part of history.
The marching songs of old
Arise once more to fill the mouths,
Of father and mother patriot
Gathered around a table of fixings,
And not around a campfire
In the cold chill of Delaware morn.
The blessings and prayers
Come as gratitude for full-bellies now,
Instead of the plea with God
A soldier makes for one more drop
Of future in his canteen's emptiness.

"Prayer Upon Hearing an Ambulance"

God, be with the one for whom the ambulance goes
Wailing for the pain that no one but he knows.
God, speed the helpers. May they find him living,
And bless the attention that they shall soon be giving.
I pray that while the man waits, You will stand by him.
Show him light and comfort as vision may slowly dim.
Lord, I pray that the ambulance reaches him in time,
But if this cannot be, lay upon him Your hand benign.
Comfort him, settle him, and take away all his fear.
I pray he goes to heaven with You, or remains safely here.

"Filibustering"

I'll filibuster
Babble, and bluster.
Stammer and stutter,
Harsh plaints I'll utter,
To the sky and sea,
And all around me.
But still You stay near.
All-knowing You hear
My wailing child song
I sing loud and long.
You listen a while,
Understanding, and smile,
But point back often
Towards Golgotha,
And make me to strain
For cause to complain.

<u>Previously Published Version Below:</u>

"Filibustering"

Babble and bluster.
Stammer and stutter,
Harsh plaints I'll utter,
To the sky and sea,
And all around me.

But still You stay near
All-knowing, You hear
My wailing child song
I sing loud and long.

You listen a while,
Understanding smile,
But look back often
Towards Golgotha,

And make me to strain
For cause to complain.

"When Comes the Hand of God"

When comes the hand of the Lord
To heavenward lift our souls
There are but few things that come
Into the forefront of our hearts
To take the throne of most revered.
Earthly treasures and blessings
Slip behind and dwindle
In the light of that certain knowledge
Glowing most esteemed and precious
At the time when we are closest
To our final and eternal destinies.
It is this knowledge that allows
A human to leave with greatest comfort,
Lacking nothing, and it consists of this:
That a man knows he has loved others,
And knows he has been loved by others.
So when someone leaves us knowing this,
And we knowing this about him also,
Let us remember the sweet music in his heart
That compels us to realize he was a blessing
Sent to us from heaven, borrowed from God,
And who now returns there with our love.

Written in Honor of Rev. John Leland,
Passed Nov. 5, 2001

"Sing a Song of Rain"

Sing a song of rain,

                      Falling from on high.

                                              The
                                          nectar of the
                                          seasons,

      Showering from the sky.

                            The cold can steal my breath

                And the chill reaches bone,

                                            Until by
                                    firelight I might
                                    sit,

Safely in my home.

                The storm will call for me,

                                        And
                                  lightning shake
                                  my spirit.

          The rain will pour from heaven;

The thunder makes me hear it.

                          When it ends, a calm will come,

                    But I sleep soundly, warm.

"Don't Fear the Wounding"

Don't be afraid of blood.
We are all human,
We must all bleed.
No man has ever lived
That hasn't bled.
No man hasn't stumped
His toe or scraped his knee
So, my child, don't fear it
When you wound yourself
Or make mistakes.
Don't curse, rant, or scream.
Clean up your toe or knee,
And just wince within.
Remember it fondly,
Greet it when,
You have forgotten where it lives
And visit it again.

"The House"

A young couple, newly married, get into their car.
The house sits at the curb and whines,
Its red-painted door shining in the morning,
'Come back to me, sit inside,
Make my hearth beat,
Preheat the oven,
Light the pilot light,
Let me live with you.'

The man tightens his lip,
And he doesn't look at the house,
Not willing to say anything of comfort to it,
Afraid his voice might shake his resolve,
But the woman cries, and she holds up her hand.
'Stay, ' she says. 'Please, don't follow us, ' she says.

They decide that a house is too big a commitment.
They leave theirs to wait on the side of Highway 280
Between Opelika and Columbus,
Like people trading in their dog for a turtle,
Or a screeching bird.

The house stays. They told it to stay.
'They'll come back, ' it says.
Its neighborhood watch sticker turns white and peels.
Nobody to watch it now.
'They'll find me, ' it says to itself.
Its head turns as the cars pass by,
And it listens for their little van
For the four doors opening wide like bird wings,
Children laughing from school and daycare.

'They'll come, ' the house says,
'There'll be a Thanksgiving here,
The overwhelming turkey-cooking smell,

Cranberry sauce, stuffing and the stuffed.
They'll be crammed wall to wall,
Bumping butt to shoulder as they try
To find their seats at the family table.

'These cars will see me in the cold November,
And they will want the warmth inside,
The orange glow of Autumn candles,
Televisions tuned to Auburn-Alabama rivalry,
Everybody's belly full.

'The drivers will open and close their fingers
By the air-conditioner ducts in their cars,
And wish they were inside,
Back in their warm beds,
Not commuting, but dreaming in my dreams.

'My family'll come and they'll bring their children home,
And in the morning: Styrofoam,
Crinkling cellophane and too many plastic pieces,
And daddy, without his slippers,
Will step on sharp little monsters in the carpet,
And jump back like spiders bit him.
Mother will be making breakfast,
Pancakes and eggy breakfast casseroles,
Eggnog staining the inside of green glasses.
The hangover of too much Christmas will settle in
And I'll sleep under the white blanket on my head, '

The house stays in Alabama near Highway 280.

The cars go by, and the house stays;
Its masters told it to stay.

The signs grow like weeds in the front yard:
First Realty, Rice Realty, Century 21,
For Sale By Owner.
Foreclosure.

The signs disappear.

Paint peels.
A few of the shingles shift.
The front steps rot.
Cats have kittens in the crawlspace.
Chimney swifts hatch in the chimney,
Bats chitter in the attic, a constant noise.
The house has forgotten their car,
The warm slide of its tires in its driveway,
The familiar jangle of keys.

The cars out on 280 have a warmth the house envies,
Commuters huddle in their coats,
Air-conditioners breathing across the radios
A man and woman chat about inconsequences and latest news.
Journey plays between blasts of hiphop and Lady Gaga.
No one looks for their bedrooms beyond the windows here again.

To the house, these are breaths of winter,
Sighs only
A bleb of life that might look,
See only ruins of memories,
And forget it in the next commercial.

The house shivers.

It waits on its own porch,
Termites and carpenter bees in its bones.
It looks over the helmet heads gathered.
It looks over the rumbling bulldozer.

'I stayed. You told me to stay, '
The house breathes out.

The Punch Clock Dragon Sighs by Jared Gullage

"Blazé"

It's a Kellogg's kind of morning,
A Band-Aid kind of hurt.
We're in a Pizza Hut family,
Living Prozac kind of lives.
Neosporin is our duck and cover.
Fox News brings our terror dose.
Asia is stuffed in Styrofoam,
Our royal jelly is microwaved.
Drink the good life sedentary.
Walk only on paths well paved.

"The City"

Clickety-clack
Go the trains
Go the dice
Go the rains
Go the mice
Go the pains.
Everything's rollin'
Growin'
People fly like flies
Without legs
Birds without eggs
Home somewhere ahead
But no homes in the city
Houses but no homes,
Mice sneaking in after hours,
Leave the lights off
I'll scurry through.
Pardon you
I was just passing through
Got someplace to get to
Edge me off the map awhile
Take me off the grid
Let me breathe on the z-axis
Let me jump from the y.
Let some other day be my
Day to fry
Hooked in at all my ports
To the electric blood of night,
No pillow drowns the siren wail
Of the city baby, the baby city
Blue-red lights
That can't get enough milk
From the single mom.
It bleeds
Not blood but ice
Crunching in the steps of strangers
Marble statues walking by each other,
Cells in the same body not talking
No one wonders.

The devil commutes,
Takes the interstate over the bridge
Into the city
Grumbles on his way
About the traffic
Never looks out his window pane
Doesn't make eye contact
Doesn't want trouble today.

"Gun In The Night"

The loud blast of joy that day
Became the strange thunder echo
Of the storm that only you heard,
And its final, mysterious lightning bolt.

I remember holding the .38,
The cold steel warming to my touch.
The stump exploded before it
Into little flying shards of almost unwood.
It was my cousin's gun,
And you were my cousin's friend,
And I remember that you had better aim than I.
It was strange to hear your name
And to shake your hand in introduction,
Not knowing that my name
Might be the last you would learn.

On a bridge somewhere outside of town
With a gun lying in the truck beside you,
The window forming a shattered picture of an eye
That watched your last moments but unable
To tell the truth to me or my cousins
About what actually happened.
It was there, only hours after I met you,
That your final mystery took place.

I prayed for you, even though you had died.
I prayed for closure and for your family,
And I prayed that God might have you.
I prayed for my cousin, too,
Whose memories of that day

Are as shattered as the glass of that night,
I also prayed for myself,
But not a selfish prayer;
I prayed to appreciate the brief meetings
And sudden partings.

Written in honor of a friend of my cousin, who by day was target shooting with us, and then that night was found in his truck, either killed by murder or by suicide.

"His Last Blink"

Brakes squeal.
Glass shatters.
The sick lurch in the middle of his stomach.
A cold wind, that feeling of falling,
The ground rushed up unstoppably.

Then, he blinked.

I want to say, but I don't know,
The next thing he saw was the little lake behind our family home,
Right at sunset when he liked to be there,
The sky the color of the cookout fire when he smashed a marshmallow in my hair
And told ghost stories about creepy old ladies "pulling my leg."
I want to say the sky is like that, and like
The Easter eggs we gathered after the big event was over at the Grandparents' house.
We threw them in the road and watched cars smash them to bits,
And their colorful shells scattered across the black asphalt like the clouds across this horizon now.

A distant soundless lightning bolt or two flash across an endless sky,
A sky that keeps going like that even beyond
Pine trees and oak trees and hickories.

I want colors for him like the sky was when the mosquitos came,
In the summer when we made our frog islands on the shores of the pond,
Which we always called a lake,
Where he taught me how to fish for carp.
We looked up in respectful reverence
In honor of the melting daylight.
The night invariably came for us then,
But never quite the same.
The sun never carved the same clouds twice.
Nor forged the same shades of orange, red, blue, or purple.

He's standing in ankle deep water.

The Punch Clock Dragon Sighs by Jared Gullage

He doesn't know how he got there.
He remembers something about feeling sick,
Trying to go home,
But it fades like a Saturday morning dream.

Out in the lake, standing on the water,
A figure of a man says:

'Come out here. The fishing's better."
Jason knows who he is,
But he didn't expect him here and now and like this.
Maybe he walks out there to him,
Impossibly,
And stands awkwardly beside him,
His hands in his pockets,
A smirk of dubious acceptance on his face.

"What happened? " he asks the figure of a man. "How'd I get here?"

'You made a mistake, but it's over with. Do you like this place?"

"Yeah. But, I don't get it. I was in a car, and…I think…."

"And now you're here, with me. Is this not where you want to be? "

"Wait. Am I…? "

"We're here. This is where we are. This is where your heart is, so here we are. I've been waiting for you."

'Waiting for me? Why?"

"I want to fish. I like to fish. Don't you? I always know the best spots."

"Oh," he says. "Well, can't you read my mind? Don't you know what I want already or something?"

"I do. I like to ask people," says the figure. "So?"

"Yeah," Jason says.

The figure hands him a pole. "It's good out here," he says.

They cast for a while. Jason looks over at the figure in the twilight.
The man beside him doesn't look like what anyone thought,
But he knew he wouldn't look like all those Caucasian paintings,
Those blue-eyed, thin-faced weirdos looking like a puppy by a table.
He knew those paintings never had him right.
But, he's still familiar, like the voice of someone who was always whispering.

They catch some fish.
Some big, some small.
They're all fighters.
They don't keep them.

Kodi and Zeus, the two Rottweiler dogs who loved him,
Come trotting across the lake as though they knew all along he was here.
They stand to either side of him, right in the water,
And Zeus looks up at him as though to say:
"This is better than a boat."

Jason pats each dog on the head. He breathes their Rottweiler stink.
Kodi snorts at him in that piggish way he used to do.

The man beside him smiles.
He wears shorts and sandals
And a t-shirt.
His hair is shorter than expected, and he sports a goatee.
Even so, Jason feels like he really knows him.
He asks the question that's hovered around him like a deer fly:

"This gonna be like one of those Sunday school things?'"

"No. Just fishing for now."

The lures splash like startled bullfrogs.
The sun never moves.

The fish don't always bite.
Sometimes the hooks snag on limbs.
Sometimes the lines get tangled.
Sometimes a fish takes the lure off the line.

The wind blows a little, just enough to make goose-bumps,
And geese fly overhead.

"I always figured...," starts Jason after a while.

"I know," the figure says.

"I'm sorry," Jason says.

"I know," the figure says. He flicks his wrist and sends his line out. He pulls at the line to tighten up the slack. He doesn't look at Jason while he's casting and reeling.

Jason gets a bass. It's not too small, about the length of a forearm, but he throws it back.

"You can keep it if you want. There are more."

"Nah. Too small."

A house waits at the top of a hill.
Lights turn on and warmth radiates like sunshine from each bright square window.

"What's that?" he asks the figure.

"That's your family coming home," the figure says. "They're getting supper ready. When we're done fishing, we'll go see who's come home tonight. Your new niece has come. A sweet girl. Your brother's child. She's eager to see us."

A pause, the man's lure dangling and dripping ringlets into the water. The rings expand from teardrops and interweave like basketwork.

"Now, your father, too. He just arrived. And your mother, too."

"Dad? Mom?"

"We'll go see them when you want."

"I Saw a Cloud Like an Angel"

A cloud shaped like an angel,
Or maybe more like an eagle.
I'm driving from Opelika to Columbus one morning.
I hoped it was an eagle,
Swooping down, claws open,
About to catch a trout
From somewhere beyond the rooftops.
I hoped it was an eagle
While it faded
...faded...
faded...
away.
I hoped it was an eagle,
Not an angel.
When angels fall,
They never rise again.

"Apologia"

I don't know if I can write this poem.
The memories I'd use to fill it
Are precious little things,
Delicate.
They don't wear words well;
They don't bear description.
I'm afraid to frame them,
For fear I'll tear the picture.
I will try and if I cry I'll know
I've written the poem I need to write.

You had sixteen hours.
You lay in my arms,
The first and last moment,
I'd cling to you under my chin.
I freed you from the tubes and wires
Holding you before I could.
They had to let you go,
Before I could.

That one time you trusted me,
I signed my name.
I signed my name.
You opened your eyes one last time.
You looked at me.
But I signed my name.
Already, you were leaving.
I found you in there,
And lost you a moment later.
The doctor shook his head,
The cold stethoscope on your bare back,
And all around me the nurses stood,
The bright hospital lights a halo,
And the world shrunk down to just us.
But I'd signed that paper.

I let you go.

I would have held you,
Kept you here,
Forever.
I held you,
And I let you go
All at once
At the same time.
I'm sorry.

I signed my name,
And lost you.
I'm sorry.
I failed you as your father.
I could not save you.
I had to let you go.
I handed you to Jesus.

I bear the pain I spared you.
Please wait for me.
Please wipe my tears away
When I hold you again,
And tell me I did right by you.
Tell me you love me,
That you've waited for me,
You've watched me,
You forgive me.
I'm sorry.

"My Peculiar Curse"

A peculiar curse in dreams and visions,
A spiritual ailment
A single good idea
Festers, grows, molds.
My mind, it says:
"'This was where it all began,'
They'll say, 'This is where he started,
One poem or story,
That one idea aptly spoken,
Destiny revealed itself,
Literature book biographies awaited.
To precede the mandatory, quintessential work,
The one all the students roll their eyes at,
Then have that line come back later.
His Henry VI Part I, or his A Boy's Will...
This is the chair he sat in, the pen he used,
The keys that clicked under the weight of his genius
Where they'll pass by, look in through
A glass-plate doorway,
When the museum is constructed,
Unlike what they did with Bradbury's house.
Some students will say they went there
When that hand of his moved just that way,
Just along that perfect inch of paper,
And scrawled out those perfect words curled just so,
To frame an idea like a pretty girl's face,
That everyone quotes now in their term papers.'"

My mind thinks these things,
Tells me to remember this first of a thousand steps.

"This is it," my mind says. "This is the day
When you began to change the world."

I write again, send my fingers to the keys again,
And now it is starting over and my mind wanders.
"This is it. This is where it began. Here. Now."

We start again.

The Punch Clock Dragon Sighs by Jared Gullage

"Frustrated Teacher Rant"

It is not "mean"
To disagree with you.
It is not rude
To deny you a privilege.
It is not disrespectful
To expect your obedience.
It is not overbearing
To make you do your work.
It is not condescending
To point out your imperfections.
It is not futile or stupid
To expect your best from you.

It is my job to help you.
It is my job to correct you.
It is my job to guide you.
It is my job to model goodness.
It is my job to influence you.
It is my job to leave you better.

It is your job to listen.
It is your job to pay attention.
It is your job to know.
It is your job to understand.
It is your job to read.
It is your job to discover.
It is your job to write.
It is your job to think.
It is your job to apply.

You are not entitled to anything.
You are not privileged above anyone.
You are not better than anyone
Until you prove yourself
First to me,
And then to the rest of humanity.
Expect nothing you have not earned.

Be thankful when such is given.
Do not boast about good fortune.
Do not brag about surviving.

Be humble when you are successful.
Be merciful when you are in charge.
Be happy when life takes nothing from you.
Be ready for when it takes something.

You are only guaranteed the past.
Go forth and put more of it behind you.

"Watching a Band At 8th And Rail Bar After Chaperoning the Prom: 2014, I Think."

Somehow, it's a red place.
Maybe it's the curtains.
The walls are white
The floor is hardwood.
Maybe it's the chair backs.
Somehow this place breathes
With that puckered lip color,
Like this place is a throat
Just behind that waitful kiss.
The ceiling dimly thinks
It reflects light,
But it hasn't had but a few drops,
What comes from candles on the tables
And slithers free from Christmas light strings
Who've never celebrated Christmas.

Somehow it is a red place.
It's gotta be the curtains.
The couches contrast it along the wall
Some kind of unnatural green
Mossy rock,
Maybe the fabric factory called it,
Before getting Chinese children to stitch it
Who've never seen moss on rocks.

The guitarist wears red.
I'll bet he works in an office.
Maybe it's that hint of red.
The bar is reddish, too,
A reddish wood glancing back.
The flash and flicker of whiskey
Clinking ice and glasses.
It flashes across a few faces
The color of aged barrels,
So the labels claim.
A few buzzy faces

The Punch Clock Dragon Sighs by Jared Gullage

They're red,
The blush of "I'm not drunk."

It's now a mystery which wants solving,
But this place is red.
It bleeds it,
The color it thinks it should bleed,
Like blood's red.
So now, I'll be red, too,
'Cause blood's alive.

Things bleed when they're alive.
This place thinks it's alive like me,
And now it's made itself red.
Somehow this place is red.

"A Ladybug Smell"

A ladybug smell
Found my nose
One Spring afternoon after school.

I knew the smell,
From childhood.
Their word for fear.
Though my clumsy fumbling hands
Had no intent to cause pain.

I let them fly off my finger and they traded
The smell for their freedom and their flight,
And I hoped I had not hurt them.
My secret wishing escorting them
From my life.

A bitter stink like
The roots of things.
It appeared in my car that Spring.

The ladybug wasn't in my car that day.
Only the smell of its fear.

"In Search of Poetry"

I went into the woods in search of Poetry,
But she is coy and good at hiding.
All I found were some trees,
Waking up and shaking with the cold
Of the November wind, toweling off
From the dew of previous night's showers.

All I heard was gossip,
Passed among chattering squirrels in their forks
To the black-feather ears of crows who laugh.
Twigs no bigger than fingers bear their mirth.

Occasionally, some wet-headed stones
Tugged my feet, nearly tripped me,
Wanting to tell me something unimportant.
They look at me from under their moss,
But forget what they wanted to say,
And sit in silent embarrassment
At having stubbed my toe pointlessly.

I looked far into the woods for Poetry,
But she is a quick runner.
She outran the deer I spooked
And sent leaping through brambles
That would tangle in my jeans for hours.
They vanish like dryads through mysterious doorways,
The portcullises of nature between the trees.
I wondered if I misinterpreted the wind,
And saw only phantom does merge with undergrowth.

Poetry must have out flown the gliding hawk,
Who came noiselessly through
The oak's gnarled and reaching fingers,
Darting straight through like a wayward arrow,

And up, up, up again.

I asked a tunneling armadillo had he seen her,
But he was too busy with his gardening to notice,
Digging up the worms and yellow jackets and snails.
When he saw me coming, knowing I wanted to talk,
He said he had housework to attend and scurried off.

Perhaps, Poetry got in the canoe and paddled across the lake
To hide behind the sun and the flaming, sunset sky.
Maybe she wished to go and pluck a bouquet made
Out of the roses and daffodils and lilacs in the heavens,
Misted with the twinkling dew of evening stars,
Knowing full well I cannot follow her.

Poetry is a teasing beauty,
One who runs giggling ahead of me,
Promising wondrous things when I catch her,
But always hiding in the places I can't go.
She runs just slow enough to hear her tread;
She is a flash of bright light,
A teasing beauty worth pursuing,
Even if I'll never ever catch her.

"Who's Never Studied Star Wars"

I cannot comprehend the mind of a man
Who says "I ain't never studied Star Wars,"
As he told me one summer day
Driving to the next lawn to mow.

I cannot picture it,
An inner forest of dreams,
Untroubled by dragons,
Where never wizard nor king
Ever sat a throne
And never starlight fell
Upon a world
But his own.

What it must be like to only know the real.
Who cannot afford a dream-fed mouth,
A desire for the unattainable,
A walk on paths in unseen sunlight?

I cannot fathom it, this depth,
Peopled by people who've only existed,
Who did things only people do,
And who sing songs about the failure
To be better than this world can make them.
To see in constellations only stars.

When such as he lay their weary heads down,
A stymied universe
Cries in the night,
Dies in the night,
Denied the food of fantasy.
Their dreams don't ever mean anything,
Never whisper life's great wisdoms
In World-Begotten weariness.

The Punch Clock Dragon Sighs by Jared Gullage

"A stove is only meant for cooking,
Never for getting burned or learning."

A man like this has never
Envisioned himself an ant's tornado
While he mows a lawn,
Never held a machete up
Called himself a warrior
Against an army of weeds.
Never thorns the hydra for a hero.

All the worries he picks up in the morning,
All the thoughts swimming round his head,
Roused like dust and minnows
To the meniscus of shallow water,
Every unsettled trifling penny spent
Are as real to him as rent.
Life is only living for such a man as this.
Life is only dying for such a man as this.

"No Music is Playing."

Poetry dwells
Within odd things
Like this:
I tell my old phone
To call my wife,
Speaking her name,
But the electric brain
Inside the thing
Says: "No Music Is Playing,"
And then denies me
The sound of her voice.

"Ancestor Homosapien"

Those first things called people,
When first benighted
Shivering in their jungles
When the last light waned
From the first day to wane
No one dared to sleep
Each screech
An enemy
In their sullen, stupid hearts.
Eyes watching
Hours passing
Without anyone
Able to name
Each feather of night
No promise or oath
To grip like branches
Until dawn slithered back
Slipping up on them
From the other direction
Like the beasts.
Those first men
Watched the sun retreat
Watched the sky wither,
Without any apologies.
They learned first fear
And then, they see second day
We are alive they say
Without words.
They had no words.
The light is back again
Without so much as a name
To call it by
To summon it back.
The warmth is back
The great light returns

The Punch Clock Dragon Sighs by Jared Gullage

What betrayal must it have been
When the night came again
And again
And again
And again
Daylight returning shamefaced
Daylight with promised friendship
Gone again
Eventually, our ancestors,
Though they begged the sun,
Pleaded with it,
Asked it: "Why do you go?"
And
"What have we done?"
Eventually, they forgot it
As their friend.
Let it go without remarking it.
They watched each day die,
Hoping to see the rest die.
Learned to live without the day,
Benighted each day by darkness,
To accept they had no choice,
No longer cared the birds flew over,
Or the sun alongside.
They named it day and night
Gave names for these everlasting
Betrayals.

"Save Them"

"Save them.
Find them wriggling
Out on the rough hide
Of summer pavement,
Their bodies hot and hurt.
They come out after rain,
Blindly searching
Squirming for damp grass
Trying to save themselves.
Butting their faces--
With relentless life--
Against unyielding stone
They would tunnel into the Earth,
If only they could find it.
Save them.
Hold them gently
In your strong, calloused hands
Let them squiggle madly
But never fall
Until you safely place them
Between the green cool
Of harmless, unsharp blades.
Save them,
Though they think
You will eat them
Or tear them apart
Or throw them.
They won't understand,
But they don't have to
Understand everything.
They cannot truly see
Or hear or even know.
But to receive mercy
Understanding is not required,
Only acceptance.
They can never thank you,
Nor in any way repay it.
Again, this is not required.
Save them,"
Said My Lord
To Jesus Christ,
My Savior.

"Love Among the Dead"

Out here, among the dead,
Is where we threatened to stir up life,
Where we tried to kindle a fire,
To keep away the cold.
We were trying to burn each other,
Temper each other with sweat,
Stoke up red flaming passion
Amidst the cold, gray marble.
We vampires, ghouls, ghosts,
Haunt the sleeping ones,
We dare flaunt our wakefulness
Dare to live.
We mean no disrespect to the dead,
But we tease them with life.
We dare them to stop us.
"Just ask, and we'll leave, but you can't,
So we won't.
Instead we'll love.
We'll kindle life.
We'll defy you while young,
And we'll wait our turn
To be voyeurs beneath the loam."

This poem was inspired by a long, lost friend from high school telling me about a night in a graveyard with her boyfriend where they were intimate together. For some reason this poem emerged from the thought of such a date.

"True Story: Nightmare 5/12/15"

In my nightmare last night,
In an apocalyptic store,
The torso of a mannequin
Wearing a letterman jacket,
His arms wrapped 'around a pole
Hooked over cross beams,
Smiled at me as he spun
Exposed eye glaring
From a skull he ought not have,
His grinning teeth and cheekbones
Shining and open-framed
By red-bloody plastic.
Round and round he rotated
With a voice like a robot,
Whose power dwindled
Like decaying isotopes,
Repeating:
"Over and over,
I pull myself over
Again and again."
What does that mean,
Dr. Freud?
Am I nuts?

"If I Did, Would You?"

I'm not going to
But if I did
Would you?
Because he said
His wife would.
I thought of us.
His wife would
If he asked her,
But I'm not asking.
I'm not going to,
But if I did
Would you?

This was vaguely inspired by a half a conversation I overheard at a school function. I added some lines, but some lines came from the conversation, too. Which ones are which, I'll never tell.

"Like Many Birds"

Like many birds
I seek a branch that doesn't shake.
I get mad at change
And oddly, I don't want to fly anymore.
At least, not always.
I want to sit still and see younger birds
Watch them rise
Hoping they'll find higher perches
Closer to the skies.

I wrote this at the graduation of some of my students (I think it was 2014 or 2015, the one before the principal made us participate in the ceremony). I thought of the students like birds, flying higher than me, leaving me, leaving the place where I've nested to work. I'm not moving on yet, but they are.

"Tea Party"

We drink tea made of air
In plastic cups with smiles on them.
I try for polite conversation,
While you wrap a blanket
Around a doll you've named
Jojo Shortcake.
You affectionately pat her head
Tell her: "It's gonna be okay."
We've told you the same thing,
And hoped we've never lied.
The hair is tangled
And a color not found in nature.
We practice polite conversation.
At least I do.
You're more honest.
You talk little.
You drink life
Made of air and imagination.
You abandon the cups
And conversation
And Jojo Shortcake.
You pick up a drum
Send a few wayward notes
Inexorably outward,
Echo a tap or two
We only hear.
"It's going to be okay,"
You echo your patriarchs.
And I hope you're not lying.

I had a little pretend tea party with my daughter, like just about any real dad would do, but this was my first as a father. We shared it with my younger daughter who can barely crawl. As a father of daughters, I have always waited anxiously for this moment. I believe fathers should have pretend tea parties with daughters. However, my mind is pulled from it by thoughts about life, worries and wonderings about career, the future, family, everything. My daughter does not really have these worries. We tell her it will be okay when she's upset about things, but when I think of saying that, I cannot tell the absolute truth to her little two-year-old mind. Life will not always be okay. And even when she echoes these words back to me, I think about them and hope they can be true.

"God's Real Language Is Poetry"

God's real language is poetry.
The esoteric curling of its letters,
Hide in plain sight a meaning
And a message none can see,
A screen of strategically placed privacy
Against all gazing eyes and none at once.
Anyone who says they can't fathom God
Is lying.
Anyone who says they can fathom God
Is lying.
The words entangle in Submission Guidelines
And read like the resumes of pharisees
And prophets.
The great works, the Great Works,
Sleep like beetle larvae
Curled in brainy dirt,
Perchance to dream forevermore.
No such thing as beforebirth,
Necessary precedents
To signal the imminence of life
Or something grand enough
To speak God's verses.
No guaranteed precursor
To noteworthiness or acclaim.
It is boldly blind
To submit one's poetry,
To the world at large, the large world,
And haphazardly whistle the tune
Of God's secret nocturne.

20 May, 2016

"A Punch Clock Dragon"

To say a teacher nests on gold,
Would be the height of insufferable,
Teachspirational
Dribbling, diatribe rubbish.

"Everyone's a butterfly."
"Everyone's special."
"All students want to learn."
"The students are our future."

Mostly these are true.
But tired.

This poem doesn't go the way I thought
At first when I titled it.
I thought it would be about punching clocks
And being magical.
A day-to-day job for an extraordinary beast,
But that's vanity.

And then that damnable image of students
Being the treasure hoard a teacher
Holds beneath his wings,
And see? There it goes again:
Wings, Beneath my wings,
My job to keep what's most valuable
Cooped up in a cave, gaining value,
As the true student grows rarer still
Until they're rescued by Graduation
I suppose, if we're going with this,
I guess this allegory could
Include the idea that sometimes
We must roast one or two of them,
But the board would frown upon that.

I keep writing this because I think it's funny,
A dragon punching a clock in the morning

The Punch Clock Dragon Sighs by Jared Gullage

And in the afternoon,
Measuring out my life by teaching about
Measuring out lives in coffee spoons.
See the allusion?
I have always liked that image and that poem.
It scared me just right.

Do I dare?

To come and do that natural thing the dragon would
Without the clock and the nagging impedimenta
Of a job and taxes and all the other whatnot.

Imagining myself a dragon
Only paints this sad image:
A creature with wings folded
Upon his back
As he hunkers down
Beneath the weight of mountains.
"Remember to submit your timesheets
Before you go a-pillaging,
If ever you go a-pillaging."

20 May, 2016

"Why Teachers Hoard"

I cleaned my classroom today.
I found that dust I wanted.
Too late now to teach
About the memories
A ball of dust can carry.
Oh well, better luck next year.

20 May 2016: Apparently, I had a moment to think that day.

"Night Clock"

I wake in darkness
And listen
The world stops.
Freezes over.
The clock in the hallway
Chimes.
Time passes,
Allegedly.
Dreams melt
And tiny baby breaths
Pant into eternity.
The clock restarts the world
Confirms all is well
Midnight vigil
The hand of change.
Sleep returns
Easy now.
All is well.
Ticking told me so.

"The Game of Ku"

Based on a Dream: 4/25/2017

She lived in an antique shop downtown,
A place not visited by many.
The power company let her keep her lights on,
And the realtors rented for free.
A charity case.
A tradition.
A duty.
Some days, outside,
Between her old store and the railroad,
On the gathered, eclectic, not-quite-sold lawn furniture,
Around a peeling-paint metal table
She opened a pack of cards with her withered hands,
And hosted a game of Ku.
I think she named the game,
And I think she made up the rules.
The name so that anyone could say it,
Even the toothless hobos,
And ancient thrift-shop ladies with hats
Who played with her.
An easy syllable to carve from the air,
With no need of teeth
Or that much for creaking jaws to do.
The rules, I think, came and went,
And people played along,
Because they liked the old lady's company
More than the cards.
I never did learn the rules.
She handed me a bunch of cards off the deck,
And she told me: "These aw you fwends.
They'll leave you eventually."
Her shaking old hands cupped my own
And dropped those cards into them
Like a sacred trust.
Then, the conversation resumed,
And the game played on,
And the homeless and the elderly,

While smiling good-naturedly,
Defeated me, hand after hand, in Ku.
The old lady told me,
"It's Ku. You'll learn it, or you won't."
She played two cards.
My sister and I visited her together
Downtown, in amongst the ragtag shops
Restored and filled to bursting,
With silvery trinkets to go on mantle shelves
And experimental beers in experimental bars
Which ran like meth labs walled in by damp alleyways.
And every time I lost, the old lady reminded me
"It's Ku. You'll learn it, or you won't."
She quickly played another two cards.
At least that round.
And the hobos and homeless, the elderly,
And my sister,
They echoed the clauses to me.
And I played and never learned the rules,
But talked and took cards,
Until the cards were no longer dealt,
And the game was over.

I dreamed of playing this game with a woman who looked remarkably like my paternal grandmother. My sister, Lauri, was in attendance. These other old people sat outside the old thrift store downtown and played this mysterious card game. I think the rules were either made up on the spot or had something to do with what was said in the conversation. I think the purpose of the game was to figure out when and why a person dropped cards into the stack. I don't even think you really looked at the cards or knew what they were. You just dropped them at a certain time in the conversation. And the conversation was never about the rules of the game.

As I pondered this dream, I loosely coined some rules for it, which almost seems anathema, even vulgar, to the players my mind invented. Basically, as people spoke, and said certain words, they dropped cards down on the table. The winner is the person who figures out each person's "rule" for dropping cards (which may be written down). So, the old lady's rule (in the dream) was something to do with pirates or the sea (though the poem does not reflect this). I made up the speech impediment in the poem to give the old lady character. But I thought, maybe she dropped her cards when she said words with 'r's' in them. For some reason, it seemed important to remember the cards were my friends. I invented the thing about "you'll learn it or you won't" for the poem (that is, it didn't happen in the dream), but that seemed to be the prevailing attitude of the game: the people playing did not really care if I learned the game or not, just that I played with them, enjoyed myself, and gave them something to do with their time.

"I am Dead, but Lesson Plans are Due"

God Forbid the Students Plan Anything.
At the computer in the classroom
The bitter, broken, worn-out husk
Of a teacher's remains remain.
His fingers, long after his jaded death,
Continue to type, dutifully,
And a spring-born fly, done with life,
Yet living still,
Bounces off air and hair
Wavering uncertainly and lands
Vaguely on the shoulder of our corpse.
The teacher's head hurts,
But he is dead.
Lesson plans are still due tomorrow.
"Be dead when you sleep."

"Elegy for Lilly Marie Gullage"

Lost: 7/6/2012
Written: 10/4/2017

Upon my chest
They lay you down
A father's unsoft chest and not
Your mother's warm embrace, and they
Unhooked you from all the wires
And patted your dying back,
The skin like silk beneath my palm,
My other hand upheld your head.
And then they brought that cursed page,
They told I'd need to sign,
And holding you with all my might.
I thought perhaps I had no hand
With which to sign the dreaded note,
That waiver that read: "I give you up,"
That awful bone-white page
With letters coffin black.
But we, my wife and I,
had chosen between this or worse,
To let you go or let you hurt.

I signed, I signed, oh God, I signed,
I signed your life away,
The same as signing checks.
Let them unhook you from this world,
So I, in father's greedy grief,
Could hold you one last time.

I leaned your head against my heart
I wept above your tiny waning strength
And wrote my name upon that page
And watched the doctor shake his head.

I've always hoped you woke again,
In heaven's holy rest
And after gone from 'neath my beard
Awoke on Jesus's waiting chest.

"Another Dream Poem: Dad CSI"

My late father retired from being a lawyer and a judge.
He became a CSI investigator and invited me
And my nephew to go out with him to the scene of a crime.
I told him we ought to take some guns out there,
And my nephew got a few from his safes and went ahead
But I frustrated Dad with indecision
I couldn't tell if I needed to take a pistol
Or a shotgun, nor why I'd even suggested anything.
We never arrived on the scene together.
I got lost driving us to it.
Then, I woke up regretting I'd dragged him back
Instead of charging off with him.

"A Joke Poem?"

Driving home one night,
Talking to myself
Like always,
But then I realized
I had to stop
And explain something
A little slower,
So I better
Understood.

10/10/2019

"Hope This Helps"

Imagine if we waited at the door,
Never sallied forth forevermore,
If we never stirred from our bed,
What makes us differ from the dead?
If we watch only from the precipice
Of mother and father's shaking nest,
What new world could ever be?
Nothing to go and nowhere to see.
Why stay tangled in our thorns,
Or stand looking up at storms?
We cannot wait nor can we stay
In the places where we'd dismay.
What good is the waking world
When, in our pasts, we stay curled?
Heaven, in us, does not despise,
the living, renewed, to newly rise.
The gift we give ones passed away:
Their lives brought on our life's day.

My sister, Lauri, asked me a question that set my mind into poetry mode. She asked me about the estate sale of my parents' belongings, how we both felt we could not keep their legacy in one piece and as a mausoleum or museum to what great people they were. Yet, we barely had the heart to dismantle everything and distribute it, much less sell anything. We both wanted to keep things just as they were before we lost our beloved parents. But we couldn't keep them, and we both knew it would drive them absolutely crazy to keep the stuff where it is and how it is.

—9/11/2019

"Woven Universe"

What does the single spider feel,
Weaving a world above the ground?
She kills and eats what visitors
Would e'er deign to come around.
And when her mate would woo her,
He must do his wriggling dance.
What is the fate he seeks to win,
But death for brief romance?
Whatever will happen to her,
Will be twanged on tiny strings.
The entirety of her life plays out
Devoid of other beings.
So did God give her a mind
Made to reach beyond her?
A will to think of distant lands?
Where she will not wander?
When one weaves a universe
To balance beneath their feet
Does one want to know aught others,
If withal is to poison and to eat?

Thought up while pumping gas.
Tuesday October 30, 2018 at the Sunoco Station
Exit 64, I-85.

"Random Tanka"

A three-legged dog
Makes triangle tracks in sand
Among the cedars

--1/31/2007

"Ivy is Convoluted"

Ivy is convoluted
Difficult to navigate
Impossible to coordinate
Never standing on its own.

A cedar is firm, resolute,
Only growing one direction,
Never changing its mind,
Always pointing to heaven.

I am ivy.

1/31/2007

"Upon Investigating A Sun-Shadow Mandala Project"

The object is a paradox in light and shadow
For at the object light and shadow
Segregate but meet each other still,
Like restrained lovers,
Palm to palm,
Peeking around a tree at one another.
The light cannot meet the dark
Without a hidden barrier between
Light never casts its own shadow,
So until something comes between,
The two can never relate.
Until there is a hiding place,
Nothing can be hidden.
Until there is a barrier
Something shoved between
Only one can exist,
And without opposition,
This desperate love does not exist
Between light and shadow.

2/7/2007

"Head over Heels"

"How does one go head over heels?"
"I don't know what you mean."
"The head is already over the heels, right?"
"I think you're overthinking it a bit."
"No, hear me out. The quite natural state of man is to stand up and have his head firmly held aloft high over his feet."
"Yes, but--"
"It would be more unnatural to say 'heels over head,' right?"
"So?"
"So, when I say I've fallen head over heels in love with you, I'm describing my natural state, the way I should be."

--2/14/2007

"If You Fall Into A River"

If you have fallen into a river
It is important to keep your feet up
And float down the current.
Rocks will tell you to stand up.
Branches will reach their hands to you.
Don't take their advice.
If you stand, the river takes you under.
If you take the branch, you may get hung.
Flow on, flow on until the river shallows
Wait and keep your feet up.

--4/18/2007

"The Wasted Light"

In a hole somewhere,
Deep underground
A hole five feet
By five feet
By five feet,
A little star shines,
A magic star,
A light shining bravely
But illumines nothing.
Worms and scorpions
Snakes and centipedes
Open pores in the walls
Of this deep oubliette
Think they have turned wrong
And retreat from that shine,
And the cold, white light
Chases them down their burrows
Seeks escape from the depths.
It is indeed very starlike
And if someone held it aloft
Above their head by night
Someone would truly confuse it
For the other stars.
It gives warmth to nothing.
It grows nothing.
No mariner sets their course
By that twinkle.
No one ponders over maps
To find it for their fortune.
If it is to be discovered,
If ever the ground is broken,
It shall be for some other motive,
Not because someone seeks it,
But by happenstance,
Long after the magic's fled
And the light has dimmed,
The wizard's interest waned,
So even the blind animal nosing
Grows familiar with the stone.

1/27/2021: I have no idea why this little thought experiment occurred to me. I feel like as this developed in my head, on my way to work this morning, it came to mean something. What, I do not know. Perhaps the meaning is as obscure as the gem in the poem.

"Let's Play"

Let's play, forget all that,
Someone will pick it up.
Let's play, just the one time,
The game I like, where you hide
And no one comes to find you.
No one understands you like me.
Let's play. One more time.
You don't need all that headache,
You don't need all that worry.
They're just jealous.
Let's play. You deserve it.
You've earned it.
Survival is work.
Let's play. You need it.
You're not doing so well.
You need to find yourself again.
You need me to help find you.
We are together. Without me
You are nothing. We're a thing.
Let's play.

"For Fields and Flowers"

She has a heart made for fields and flowers
And hair for the wind to ply.
Her eyes composed of burning sunsets
And skin to reflect the sky.
She laughs like one who's liberated,
Who childishly travels on clear paths.
Never to find herself upbraided,
By cloudbroke golden shafts.

"A Window Casement"

I want a window casement
By the rain at night
Where I scratch my thoughts
And fictions upon my curled-up knees.

"But, I love…"

We stood by each other at the party.
We'd only just met, but we
Could turn our sneers outward
Together. They didn't understand.
We laughed together
At other people's laughter.

"Let's hang out," we said.
"Sure," I said, "Nothing better."
At work, eyes propped up.
Coffee. Nodding at inanity.
"Let's hang out," I said.
"Work's getting to me."

We share the rent now
Same ol' crap on T.V.
We make the same comments
About the news every night.
"They oughta...."
"Man, if I had that kind of money…"
We hang out.

One day, we're not together.
I call and call, look for signs.
"Where are you," I text.
I haunt our old spots, lurking.
Work never calls anymore.

Saw an old friend
But didn't speak.
She'd tell me I look terrible.
Or worse, she wouldn't.
She'd tell me I looked great.
Nod at my decisions
How I'd dented my couch
Smile at how my power flickers
Every month

And gently slide her child
To the other side of her.
The old friends do that now.

My new friend and I
Reconvene out behind the Red Cross.
Volunteers don't carry handcuffs.
We talk about how strong we are
How we're making it.
How things are just fine.
I miss my old couch.

"Artists Unlike Me"

When I picture artists unlike me
I see them on a balcony by the sea.
A darkness edged in warmth behind
Family near inside.
I picture lamps looking over,
Lighting up a reader's shoulder.
A musing place, perfect made
To enter in, let worries fade.
I envy their simple seeming life,
Their perfect escape and lack of strife.

Made in the USA
Columbia, SC
10 November 2024